For Ben, Ted and Will
A&C Guillain

EGMONT
We bring stories to life

First published in Great Britain 2016 by Egmont UK Limited
This edition published 2018 by Dean,
an imprint of Egmont UK Limited,
The Yellow Building, 1 Nicholas Road, London, W11 4AN
www.egmont.co.uk

ISBN 978 0 6035 7583 9

70184/001

Printed in Malaysia

A CIP catalogue record for this title is available from the British Library.

TREATS FOR A T-REX

Adam & Charlotte Guillain   Lee Wildish

EGMONT

A boy called George had a staggering thought,
That a **T. rex** could still be ALIVE!

So he built a **hang glider** and packed up his bag,

With the tools he would need to survive.

George looked at his map and called, "Trixie - let's go!
We'll need all of your tricks when we're there."

Then his dog did a **backflip** and jumped in the bag,
And the friends glided off through the air.

They soared over cities and far out to sea,

Till a **strange island** came into view!

An **enormous volcano** rose out of the mist

And down to its summit George flew.

When they came in to land, Trixie
spotted a **ball**
And she leapt out of George's backpack.
But what she unearthed was a very
large egg
That suddenly started to . . .

CRACK!

"It's a **dinosaur egg!**
shouted George, "and it's HUGE!"
Trixie barked as it rolled all about.
Could it be that a **T. rex** was
going to hatch?

No - a pterosaur baby popped out!

The **pterosaur's mother**

swooped down with a squawk,

George knew he had only one chance.

"Quick, Trixie," he shouted,

"Let's teach them a **trick . . .** "

And the pterosaurs learned how to **dance!**

But as George rewarded them all with a **treat**,
From above came a strange munching sound.
"Trixie - look out!" shouted George in alarm . . .

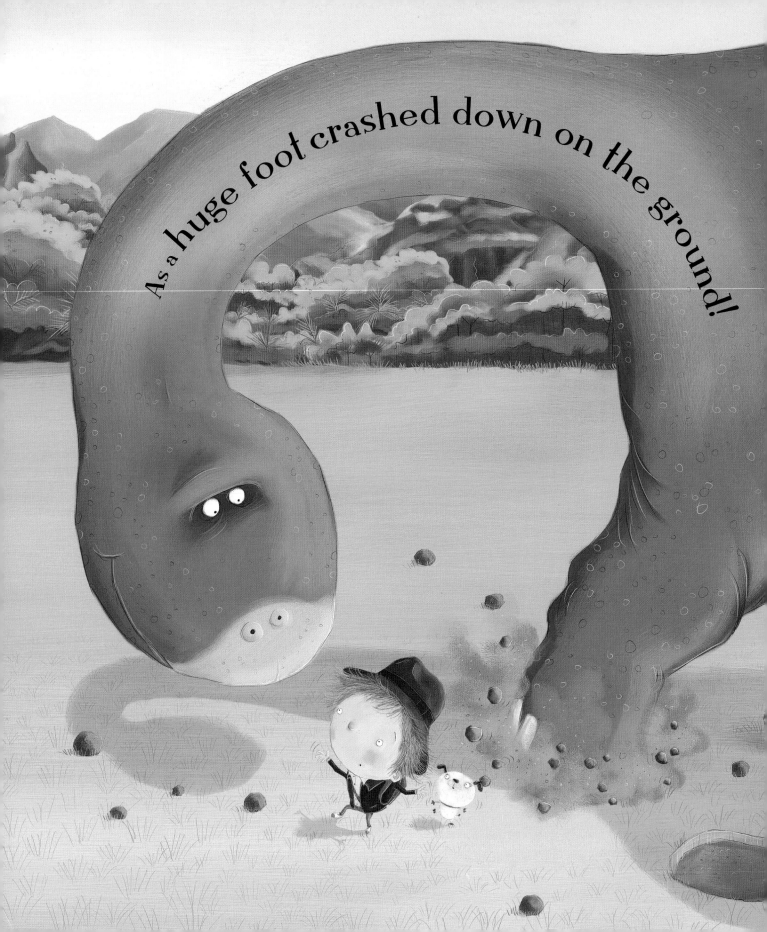

As a huge foot crashed down on the ground!

"A massive diplodocus!"

George gasped in awe.

Then he gulped as it lifted its leg.

As quick as a flash, George

called out to his dog . . .

Who taught it to
sit up and beg!

"These dinosaur tricks are **amazing**,"

cheered George,

And diplodocus grinned as it sat.

But just as the thrill of success

made George smile . . .

A tail hit the mud with a SPLAT!

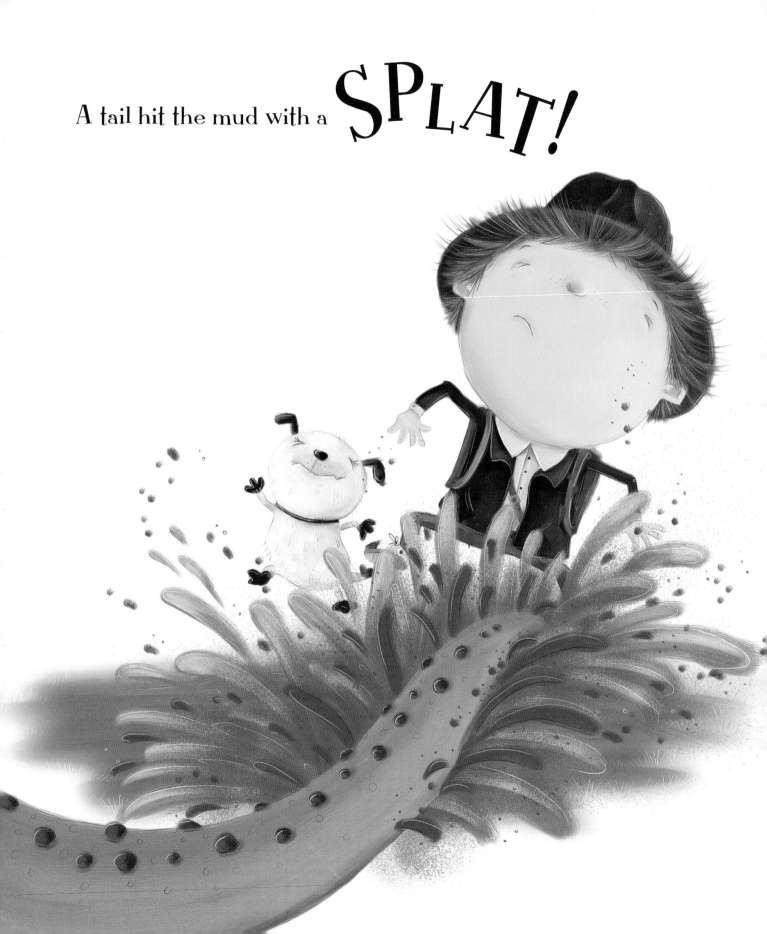

A grumpy triceratops glared down at George,
Then widened its jaws at full stretch!
George picked up some sticks and he looked at his dog –
"Come on, Trixie!" he said . . .

"Let's play **fetch!**

Triceratops playfully joined in the game,

But, fed up, George slumped to the ground.

He'd come on this mission to find a T. rex...

Then he heard a **loud stampeding sound!**

And into the clearing there burst a great herd
Of **terrified** small dinosaurs.

"Something scary is coming!"
George called to his dog,
Then he heard the most terrible...

ROAR!

"A T. rex at last!"

shouted George with a whoop,

Then it opened its jaws for a snack.

"It thinks we're for **dinner!**" George stammered in fear.

Just then Trixie rolled on to her back.

"Really?" George asked, as he tickled her tum,

How he hoped that her plan wouldn't fail . . .

The **T. rex** just snorted and tilted its head,

Before . . .

...rolling and wagging its tail!

"Clever Trixie!" cried George, as he threw her a treat,

Then he lifted his hand and said "SIT!"

The T. rex obeyed and George had an idea,

"I know what to do - let's train it!"

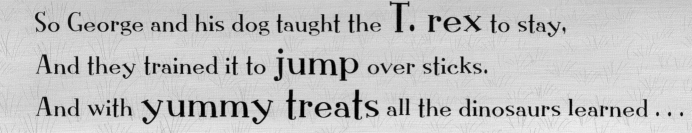

So George and his dog taught the T. rex to stay,
And they trained it to jump over sticks.
And with yummy treats all the dinosaurs learned . . .

How to do perfect **prize-winning tricks!**